URGENCY EMERGENCY!
Trapped Beetle

D0268927

For Sylvie & Mike, with all my love

Bloomsbury Publishing, London, Berlin and New York

First published in Great Britain in 2009 by Bloomsbury Publishing Plc
36 Soho Square, London, W1D 3QY

Text and illustrations copyright © Dosh Archer 2009
The moral right of the author/illustrator has been asserted

All rights reserved
No part of this publication may be reproduced or transmitted by any means, electronic,
mechanical, photocopying or otherwise, without the prior permission of the publisher

A CIP catalogue record of this book is available from the British Library

ISBN 978 0 7475 9760 5

Printed in Singapore by Tien Wah Press

1 3 5 7 9 10 8 6 4 2

All papers used by Bloomsbury Publishing are natural, recyclable products made from
wood grown in well-managed forests. The manufacturing processes conform to the
environmental regulations of the country of origin

www.bloomsbury.com/childrens
www.urgencyemergency.com

URGENCY EMERGENCY!
Trapped Beetle

Dosh Archer

ROTHERHAM LIBRARY SERVICE	
B510985	
Bertrams	24/03/2010
JF	£4.99

LONDON BERLIN NEW YORK

It was a quiet morning at City Hospital. Doctor Glenda was making some important notes and Nurse Percy was making the beds.

Just then the ambulance arrived.

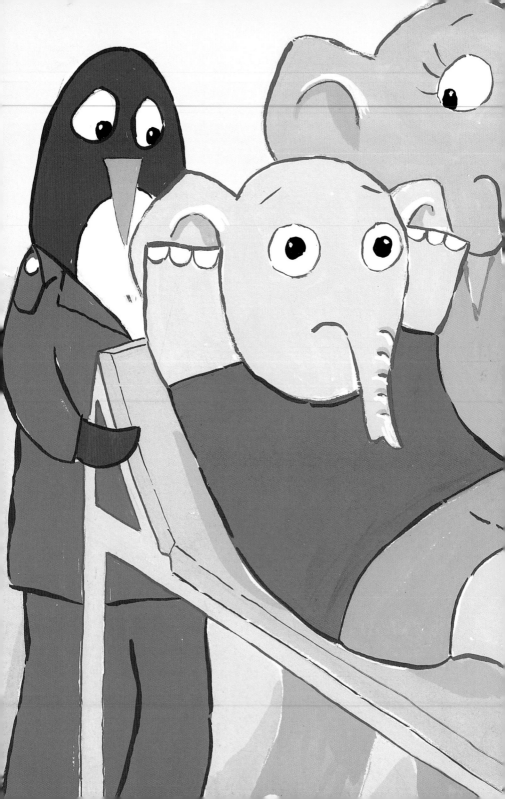

'Upset elephant! We have an
upset elephant here!'

Little Elephant was looking very worried. His mother was with him. 'I keep hearing a voice in my head!' Little Elephant cried.

'Thinking there is a voice in your head must be very upsetting,' said Nurse Percy.

A voice was coming from
Little Elephant's ear . . .

'There *is* a voice in his head,' said Doctor Glenda. 'We need some tests. I will carry them out myself.'

Doctor Glenda shone a light into Little Elephant's ear so she could have a good look.

The voice shouted . . .

It's too bright!

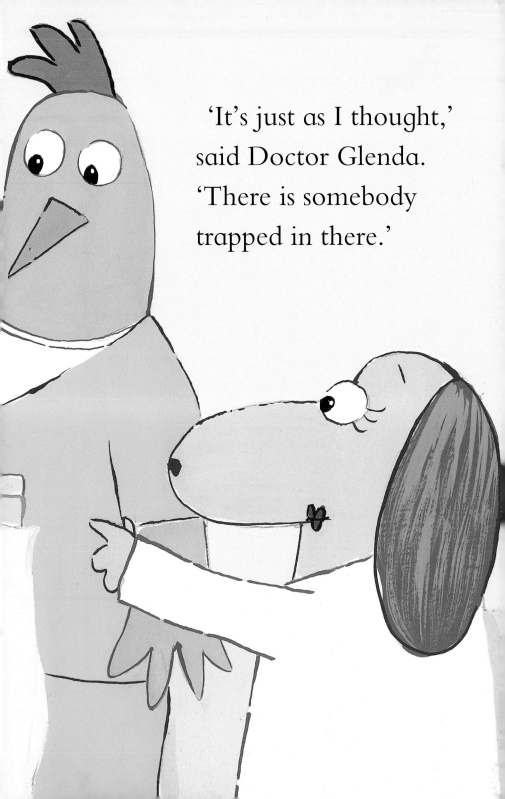

'It's just as I thought,' said Doctor Glenda. 'There is somebody trapped in there.'

The voice called out again . . .

'Aaargh!' cried Little Elephant.
'Get it out!'

'What were you doing before you started hearing the voice, Little Elephant?' asked Nurse Percy.

'I was just lying in the grass looking at the clouds,' said Little Elephant.

Beetle shouted . . .

I was just going for a walk when I stumbled into a long, dark tunnel.

'Beetle must have crawled into Little Elephant's ear by mistake,' said Doctor Glenda.

Doctor Glenda tried shouting directions to Beetle. But that didn't work.

Left! Right!
Left again!

'There is only one thing left,' said Doctor Glenda. 'I will carry out the procedure myself.'

'Is it dangerous?' asked Little Elephant.

'Only for Beetle,' said Doctor Glenda.

Beetle did not like the sound of that . . .

Nurse Percy brought a tray with a jug of water, some cotton wool and a towel.

'Doctor Glenda will pour the water into your ear,' explained Nurse Percy,

'and as the water rises,
Beetle will too, until he is
washed out of your ear.'

Doctor Glenda started to pour.
Beetle shouted . . .

I can't swim!

Round and round the water swished in Little Elephant's ear, until his whole ear was full of water. Round and round went Beetle, spluttering and gasping, until – whoosh! – he was washed out and splashed on to the floor.

'His heart isn't beating and he isn't breathing!' cried Nurse Percy.

'Step aside!' cried Doctor Glenda. 'I must breathe some air into his lungs and pump his heart until he starts breathing himself.'

Everyone watched as Doctor Glenda worked on Beetle. Would he make it?

Cough! Cough! Beetle started breathing again!

Little Elephant's ear was fine. Mrs Elephant was able to take him home that day.

Beetle had to stay in overnight so Nurse Percy could keep an eye on him, but the next day Doctor Glenda said he could go home.

'How can I ever thank you enough,' said Beetle.

'All in a day's work,'
said Doctor Glenda.

Thanks to Doctor Glenda and her team, Little Elephant and Beetle were fine. It was another good job done at City Hospital.

Enjoy more madcap first readers in the
URGENCY EMERGENCY! series . . .